Billy Goat and His Well-Fed Friends

Billy Goat and His Well-Fed Friends

by Nonny Hogrogian

An I CAN READ Book

HARPER & ROW, PUBLISHERS

NEW YORK, EVANSTON, SAN FRANCISCO, LONDON

Jx

9/73

BILLY GOAT AND HIS WELL-FED FRIENDS

Library of Congress Catalog Card Number: 72-76497
Trade Standard Book Number: 06-022565-3
Harpercrest Standard Book Number: 06-022566-1
FIRST EDITION

Billy Goat and His Well-Fed Friends

Billy Goat lived on a farm.

Billy Goat ate in the morning
and played in the yard.

Billy Goat ate at noon
and played in the yard.

8

Billy Goat ate in the evening
and played in the yard.

Then he slept all night.

Billy Goat woke up

the next morning

and began again.

He ate and played,

and he ate and slept.

But each new day,

Billy Goat ate more

and played less.

Billy Goat was getting fat!

One morning

the farmer said to his wife,

"Billy Goat will soon

be ready for us to eat."

Billy Goat heard him.

"Not if I can help it!"

he said.

Billy Goat rammed his horns

against the gate.

And he ran away!

Billy Goat passed the farm
where the chubby pig lived.

"Good morning, Pig,"

said Billy Goat.

"Good morning to you,"

said the chubby pig.

"You are looking well-fed

this morning,"

said Billy Goat.

"Yes, that is because

my farmer likes me,"

said the chubby pig.

"No, that is because

the farmer

would like to eat you,"

said Billy Goat.

"Not if I can help it!"

said the chubby pig.

"Come with me,"

said Billy Goat.

"We can build

a house in the woods

and live in peace together."

The chubby pig

was happy to join him.

The two friends

began to look for

their new home.

On the way

they met a plump goose.

22

"Good morning, Goose.

How well you look,"

said Billy Goat.

"Thank you,"

said the plump goose.

"I wish I felt well.

My farmer feeds me so much

that I feel too full."

"He must be getting ready

to eat you,"

said Billy Goat.

"Not if I can help it!"

said the plump goose.

"Come with us,"

said Billy Goat.

"We can build

a house in the woods

and live in peace together."

The plump goose

was happy to join them.

The three new friends

went on to look for

their new home.

Before long

they saw a round rooster.

28

"Good morning, Rooster,"

said Billy Goat.

"How are you this morning?"

"Not too well, thank you,"

he said.

29

"My farmer gave me
too much grain,"
said the round rooster,
"and I ate it all up."
"I guess he wants
to eat you,"
said Billy Goat.

"Not if I can help it!"

said the round rooster.

"If you come with us,"

said Billy Goat,

"we can build

a house in the woods

and live in peace together."

The round rooster

was happy to join them.

The four new friends

went on to look for

their new home.

A lazy lamb

was crossing their path.

"Good morning, Lamb,"

said Billy Goat.

"Is something wrong?"

"No," said the lazy lamb,

"but my farmer

feeds me too well.

My body is getting too heavy

for my thin legs."

"The farmer will be ready

to eat you soon,"

said Billy Goat.

"Not if I can help it!"

said the lazy lamb.

"If you come with us,"

said Billy Goat,

"we can build

a house in the woods

and live in peace together."

The lazy lamb

was happy to join them.

And the five new friends

went on to look for

their new home.

They found

a clearing in the woods,

and they began to work.

They dragged logs

from all corners

of the forest.

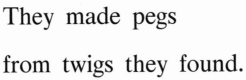

They made pegs

from twigs they found.

41

They built up the logs
and stuffed the cracks
with mud and moss.

They hammered in the pegs,

and they made a roof

with the bark of the trees.

Soon their house was ready,

and the five new friends

moved in.

But something

was about to happen

that was not very peaceful.

Two wolves

lived in a den nearby.

The wolves decided

to have some fun

with their new neighbors.

The first wolf

hopped in the window

to surprise them.

The five friends jumped

before the second wolf

could make a move.

Billy Goat

rammed the wolf

with his horns.

The wolf fell on his head.

The chubby pig

bit his tail.

The plump goose

pecked at his ear.

The round rooster

flapped his wings

and made a horrible noise.

56

And the lazy lamb

butted him

out of the door.

The first wolf

told the second wolf,

"These are neighbors

I do not care

to see again."

The second wolf agreed.

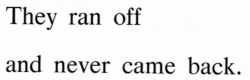

They ran off

and never came back.

Billy Goat and his friends

sat down to supper.

There was less to eat

in their house in the woods,

but they lived in peace together.